For Captain Caleb and MadMax — J.K.C.

For Megan and Natalie, my favorite little Riverkeepers. — M.D.R.

Osprey Adventure

Jennifer Keats Curtis

illustrated by
Marcy Dunn Ramsey

Tidewater Publishers
Centreville, Maryland 21617
www.cmptp.com

A bright flash of color caught Pete's eye.

As dad drove over the bridge, Pete spied a blue trash bag poking out among the big sticks stacked untidily above Channel Marker 8.

"An osprey nest!" he said, recognizing the huge messy pile of limbs, "But why is there trash in it?"

"While making nests, ospreys pick up whatever they can get their talons on," dad said. "They like to frame the outside of the nest with hard sticks, but they like to make the inside soft. Ospreys gather and lay down soft grasses and leaves. They also pick up garbage that they think will make a nice lining for their nestlings. Besides bags, nests might contain old teddy bears, dolls, and dog toys, used paper plates, even clothes that people have thrown away. Worst of all, many nests contain fishing line, balloon ribbon, or kite string. These materials can be dangerous to the birds. They can twist around chicks and adults, tying them down so that they can't move or eat."

Worried about the trash in the osprey's nest, Pete and his dad, whom everybody called Doc, decided to get in their boat and go around to the channel marker for a better look.

Using binoculars, Pete focused on the nest. He could see the blue bag flapping like a flag. A shredded black plastic bag was also snarled among the jumbled sticks on one side.

A dirty yellow braided rope trailed from the other side. One big stick was wrapped in purple string, and an orange blob was a balloon that had popped and melted. But what most bothered Pete was the big wad of tangled green fishing line near the top of the nest.

Suddenly, Pete nearly dropped his binoculars. He heard a loud, shrill call: *Shook. Shook. Shook. Shook. Shook.*

The big brown bird with the white belly looked like another bird of prey, an eagle. But this raptor's wings flapped slowly. Pete noticed a bend at the bird's elbow and the black wrist mark that looked like a bracelet.

He was sure it was an osprey.

The bird circled. Pete saw a small fish in his talons. Ospreys are great fishermen. They are often called fish hawks. Their rough, curved feet are perfect for catching and holding slippery fish, which is just about all they eat. They dive, feet first, into the water, then quickly snap their talons around a fish and hold it tight before carrying it off.

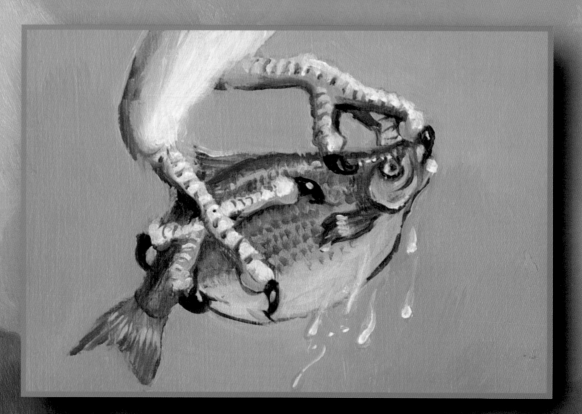

As Pete adjusted his binoculars, the osprey circled the nest twice, flapped his wings slowly, and hovered like a helicopter. He plunked down onto the side of the nest, next to the mother osprey.

She stood up and flapped her wings, then snatched the fish away from the father. He flew away, perhaps to look for more lunch. Using her razor-sharp beak, the mother osprey tore the fish into bite-sized pieces for the nestlings.

As Doc steered the boat closer to the marker, Pete saw a black-and-white speckled head pop up over the top of the sticks. The nestling's curved black beak opened to take the fish from its mother. Pete and his dad became worried. Usually there are two to three chicks in a nest. Could other babies be in that nest? Could they be tangled in the line?

While Pete tied a line to the marker so that the boat would not drift away, Doc looked up the battered, rusted metal marker. He saw more trash—a shredded black plastic bag and red sticky tape—and the bundled fishing line that had concerned Pete. He needed to climb up the marker and look inside the nest.

Although laws do not allow most people to climb markers or even touch ospreys, Doc is a biologist (wildlife expert) who works with the birds. From his boat, Doc often visits markers, pilings, buoys, and platforms along the river. He checks osprey nests for trash, especially fishing line and balloon string that can hurt adults and nestlings. Because he is studying and helping these raptors, Doc has special permission to climb the markers and to touch the birds when necessary.

As Doc began climbing the ladder, the mother osprey peered down at him with banded, yellow eyes. She flapped her wings and ruffled her dark-brown feathers. She tried to look as big as possible so that Doc would go away, but he continued climbing. Abruptly, the mother osprey hunkered down, then flew away, shrieking loudly. She nervously continued circling the nest, screeching, but Doc ignored her. He needed to see if that line was in her nest.

Just over the top of the ladder, Doc saw the young bird who had eaten the fish. The nestling also tried to scare Doc away. He ruffled the feathers on the back of his head. They looked spiky. While he was too young to fly, he tried to flap his speckled wings. He also squawked loudly, but Doc wasn't afraid. He had work to do.

By now, Doc could see that there was indeed fishing line in the nest. It was tangled around the other nestling's beak. What a mess! The young bird lay motionless on one side of the nest and looked at Doc with his orange eyes. His sibling continued to cry loudly and fluff his feathers, showing that he was upset.

Moving slowly and carefully, Doc pulled a knife out of his pocket. He kneeled on the platform and leaned over the nest. He spoke soothing words to the frightened baby birds. "Don't worry, little guys, everything will be fine," he said.

The osprey mother continued orbiting her nest, calling to her nestlings. Doc gently began pulling the twisted line and cutting cautiously at the knots. He pulled away one piece of line after another until the baby's beak was completely free.

Doc breathed a sigh of relief. The nestling would be fine. Doc put that snarled mess in his pocket. He climbed back down the ladder to Pete, who was anxiously waiting at the bottom.

Together they watched the shrieking mother osprey circle the marker twice more. Then she settled back into the nest to check on both babies. She turned her bright yellow eyes toward Pete and Doc and shrilled *shook, shook,* as if to thank them for their help.

Pete and Doc went away happily. Soon, the father osprey would return to the nest with another fish, and both nestlings would get another meal. By September, the baby would be able to migrate south with the rest of his family.

Pete slung his arm around Doc and the two headed for home, glad that their family had helped the osprey family.

Dear Readers,

   Ospreys are among the most recognized birds in the Chesapeake Bay area. Several years ago, these incredible animals almost became extinct because they were exposed to a pesticide. Fortunately, the fish hawks made a remarkable comeback after the pesticide was banned. Today, they can be found on all continents, except Antarctica, proudly perched on the sides of their big nests of jumbled sticks.

   However, these fishing birds are still in danger because they like to make their nests soft for their babies. They will pick up any trash that looks like it might make a comfortable cushion. They love to grab fishing line, ribbon, and trash bags to make a pillow for their babies, but these materials can get caught in ospreys' wings and talons. This trash can hurt, and even kill, these wonderful birds.

   YOU can help keep these birds safe in four ways:

- When you see trash on the ground, pick it up and throw it away, so that it does not end up in any bird's nest.
- Safely put away, throw away, or recycle unused fishing line, tackle, and hooks so that no birds or other animals will become entangled like the birds in the story.
- If you plan on throwing away fishing line, place it in a trashcan and close the lid tightly.
- Do not throw any trash, especially plastic or pieces of plastic, into the water.

Do your part to keep ospreys safe!

For more information, please visit www.ospreybook.com.

Sincerely,

Jennifer Keats Curtis